# Make Music

## by Ted Dewan

David Fickling Books

OXFORD · NEW YORK

Round the corner,
Not far away,
Bing goes BONGO BANG all day.

Hello
Bing.

Hello
Flop.

# Let's make music.
## What shall we play?

rice tub

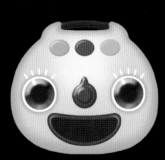

keys

music box

bell

tube

Pick one!

Rice goes *shaka shaka*

beep!

Keys go
jingle
jing

# A bell goes
## *dingle ding*

Bing goes

BINGO!

BO

Bing goes

**BINGO!**
**BONGO!**
**BANG!**

Don't go bongo, Bing.

Bing goes

**BINGO!
BONGO!
BANG!**

Don't go
bongo,
Bing.

!

No, Bing! No! Don't go...

Oh
NO.

Poor music box is
broken.

Maybe we can
mend it, Bing.

And then, together...

# Making music.

## It's a
## Bing Thing.